Snow Day!

For Carolyn Cope, who really needed a snow day and set my mind in motion
And for my aunt Betty Gaither, who always made snow days memorable in my childhood

—L. L.

For Andy, Pete, and (especially) Osia

—A. G.

Published by
PEACHTREE PUBLISHERS
1700 Chattahoochee Avenue
Atlanta, Georgia 30318-2112
www.peachtree-online.com

Text © 2007 by Lester L. Laminack
Illustrations © 2007 by Adam Gustavson

First trade paperback edition published in 2010

Art direction by Loraine M. Joyner
Book and cover design by Melanie McMahon Ives

The illustrations were created in oils on paper

Printed in March 2010 by Imago in Singapore
10 9 8 7 (hardcover)
10 9 8 7 6 5 4 3 2 1 (trade paperback)
10 9 8 7 6 5 4 3 2 1 (hardcover with CD)

Library of Congress Cataloging-in-Publication Data

Laminack, Lester L., 1956-
  Snow day / written by Lester L. Laminack ; illustrated by Adam Gustavson.
-- 1st ed.
    p. cm.
  Summary: Someone is very, very excited about the possibility of missing school due to snow, and plans a whole day of sledding, building forts, reading, and sipping hot chocolate rather than going to school for that test on chapter ten.
    ISBN 13: 978-1-56145-418-1 / ISBN 10: 1-56145-418-4 (hardcover)
    ISBN 13: 978-1-56145-553-9 / ISBN 10: 1-56145-553-9 (trade paperback)
    ISBN 13: 978-1-56145-554-6 / ISBN 10: 1-56145-554-7 (hardcover with CD)
  [1. Snow--Fiction. 2. Teachers--Fiction. 3. Schools--Fiction.] I. Title.
  PZ7.L1815Iaan 2007
  [E]--dc22
                    2007003088

Snow Day!

Written by
Lester L. Laminack

Illustrated by
Adam Gustavson

PEACHTREE
ATLANTA

Did you *hear* that?

Did the weatherman just say what I
thought he did?

Did he say…

SNOW?

Oh please, let it snow. Lots and lots of snow.

Look at the sky. I can feel it in the air. We're getting snow tonight for sure.

Just imagine...so much snow, even the buses can't go.

No—so much snow even the *teachers* can't go.

Yes! A snow day.

You know what that means?

No alarm clock ringing.

No one saying, "Time to get up."

No one shouting, "Hurry or you'll be late!"

No school!

I can't wait.

Tomorrow we'll have a PJ day.

We'll pile on the sofa and snuggle
under that old blue blanket.

We'll sip hot chocolate from giant
snowman mugs.

We'll stay inside, warm and cozy, while the
snow drifts down in soft white heaps.

Look out the window. It's spitting snow!

I hope it snows a foot deep.

I hope the snow piles up to the top of the steps.

I hope there's so much snow we can't even
open the door.

No
school
for
sure!

I *need* a snow day—
a day to play outside,
a day to read my new book,
a day to watch TV.

Did you hear that?

The weatherman said it's getting colder.
Maybe we'll get TWO snow days.

We've gotta get ready. Where are those fuzzy mittens?
What about the snow boots?

We can build a snow fort down by the walk.
This time let's make it two feet—no, four feet—tall,
and stack up a zillion snowballs inside.

Whoa, look at that sky! Snow is falling
like a bazillion goose feathers.

Yippee! Wonderful, amazing, we-can't-go snow.

Where'd we put the sleds?

Come on, help me bring them up.

We'll go sledding in Mrs. Cope's field. The sleds will
shoot down that hill.

I know, I know. We should go to bed.
Tomorrow's a big snow day.

Goodnight, everyone.
Sleep tight, everyone.
We're building a snowman tomorrow…

Say, what's that noise? Is it morning already?

Do I hear kids on the street? We've gotta get out

there and build our fort!

Open the curtain—see what's going on.

Look at all those kids bundled in coats…

and hats…

and mittens…

and boots…

and…

BOOK BAGS?

What
happened
to all
that
SNOW?

Yikes! We have to hurry. There's no time to waste.

Brush your teeth.
Wash your face.
Comb your hair.

Throw on your clothes!

We've gotta go.

WAIT!

I forgot my books.

WAIT!

Where are the keys?

Zoom-zip-scoot. Pile in the car.

I
CAN'T
BE
LATE!

I'm the teacher!

Drat! I really needed a snow day.